The
InnKeeper

✹

J. Sid Raehn

📖 My Story Publishing, Inc.

26 Emerald Crest Dr.
PO Box 3005
Cashiers, NC 28717
(850) 668-5846
Web Site: MyStoryPublishing.com
Email: MyStoryPub@aol.com

For information regarding speaking engagements call:
(404) 219-8750

FIRST EDITION

© 2002, J. Sid Raehn
All rights reserved including the right of reproduction in whole or in part in any form.

Library of Congress Cataloging-In-Publication Data has been applied for.

This book is mostly a work of fiction. Names were drawn from the Old and New Testaments, but the characters, outside of Mary, Joseph, and the Christ child, are the products of the author's imagination and are used fictitiously. Caleb's prayer to the Christ child is from the Episcopal Book of Common Prayer.

Illustrations by Bob Tummolo

Manufactured in the United States of America

ISBN 0-9709635-0-5

20 19 18 17 16 15 14 13 12 11 10 9

DEDICATION

To Pat and Maggie
who believe in angels
and to
Marty
who was one
1921 - 1995

The InnKeeper

PROLOGUE

Centuries of undisputed evidence prove that the events featured in the story you are about to read could have happened exactly as they are described on the following pages. Miracles, dreams, and angels have been with us since Adam was first placed on the earth. Miracles do happen, and are happening somewhere this very day. Our understanding of them is just as difficult today as it was 2,000 years ago. But our struggle to comprehend the mystery does not negate the fact that miracles do happen, dreams of prophetic proportion do occur, and that angels are all around us, just as they were on the first Christmas in Bethlehem.

In the *Pensées*, Blaise Pascal wrote, "Life is a dream, a little more coherent than most." He also stated the case of faith in the form of a wager, a coin flip. Pascal challenged us to wager our dream: Either God exists, or he doesn't. To the believers, by betting on the existence of God, our life dream gains a rich tradition in our brief time in the sun and a strong value system, and we hope against hope, for a life beyond. The non-believer, who rejects the idea of God, is betting on a zero, which, in the roulette of human experience, has no payoff here or hereafter.

The truth is we will never be sure we are right until our dream has ended. But, just suppose…

The InnKeeper

When Nathan, the owner of Bethlehem's only inn, had concluded his trip to the market, he was still exhausted and was now injured. While walking back to the inn, he was even more agitated than he had been before he left. He was raw from shoulder to foot. For the moment, he had forgotten all about the dream he had the night before.

The census business had been enormously profitable for Nathan and the other merchants in Bethlehem. The masses were seeking accommodations, but the complaints that went along with his overflowing guest lodge were many. Nathan was nearly stretched to his physical and mental limits. His help at the inn consisted of himself, Leah (the girlfriend of his son, Caleb, who was away at the academy), an orphan boy named Jonathan who worked for food and a place to sleep, and Nathan's devoted wife, Martha.

Nathan needed at least three more employees to make things work smoothly at the inn during the season of the Caesar's census order, but Bethlehem's labor pool was drained. Every able-bodied, unemployed citizen who could walk, had already been retained by the local full-time merchants and by the horde of traveling salesmen who came into town by caravan.

The region's rank and file began to hit the city the day after the official reading of the order. After hearing the word regarding the Caesar's decree that all of Syria would be counted, those living closest to the city entered the gates within the first few hours of the announcement. There was some soft grumbling, considering that even the village idiot could recognize the tax consequences of the mandate. For the most part, however, there was little opposition.

Those living in and near Bethlehem didn't require much. They came into town for just the day, performed their duty by registering with the Roman officials, and left to return home shortly thereafter. Before leaving, most quickly waded through the market to see the caravan merchants' new offerings. Most of the local registrants returned to their homes before nightfall.

Camel trains and mules, loaded with materials and merchandise, followed the first few citizens so closely into the city that city dwellers wondered if merchants had received word of the census before its official reading. Perhaps they had been on their way to the city before its announcement. On the first day of the census, the caravan merchants began setting up their tents and stalls in Bethlehem Square, just one alley and four short blocks from Nathan's inn. At first, the

J. Sid Raehn

city's mood was cautious, yet festive. Even the Roman officials exchanged pleasantries. But as Syrian citizens continued to pour into the city and the city became deadlocked with long lines at the well, a half-day's wait at the baths, and food shortages, faces began to blur and tempers replaced the merriment.

The marketplace became crowded with people of all ages and occupations. They were hurrying along as if every moment was of consequence to them, and as if it were impossible that anyone's business could be as important as their own.

On the fourteenth day, the Nazarenes from Galilee, some eighty miles away, were trickling in. Most were on foot, and all were tired and in need of a place to stay.

In anticipation of complaints from their guests, Nathan, Martha, and Jonathan had hung heavy canvas tarps in the courtyard between the iron gate that split the wall and the inn's entrance. They had hoped to lend a sense of security to those who turned to the inn for a place to sleep after all of the indoor rooms were promised.

The tarps provided more than a sanctuary from the street urchins, the beggars, and those who prey on the sleeping. They also offered some refuge from the heavy dew that fell at night on the hill that held the city dank just before each sunrise. However, they did little to muffle the voices and the cacophony of noises in the night that crisscrossed and merged like the flames dancing in the cook fires.

The inn's guests prepared their own meals on open fires in one of four designated areas set aside just for cooking. Their gear and animals–the animals that were lucky enough to get in before the city gates were closed to them–were placed in open stalls behind the building. Jonathan's job was to see that the water buckets were filled twice a day and that the troughs were filled with grain each morning. He also made sure that the travelers had plenty of firewood to cook with in the courtyard's open area. At the end of the day, Jonathan received his meal and a place to stay in one of the stalls.

When the inn was full, as it was on this occasion, the stalls were used for guests. The animals had to be removed and tethered to posts behind the stable yard. On these days, Jonathan had to sleep wherever he could find space on the ground, usually under a large gopher tree between the stall area and the side of the inn.

At first, Nathan was overjoyed that he could charge twice the price of a single room for an old blanket, while they lasted, and a place on the ground under the canvas tarps. But given the inn's cramped quarters, the dissonance of night noise, and the grouses and complaints of the guests, the census event was beginning to wear on Nathan and his small staff.

Nathan had saved the inn's better rooms for the rich merchants who set up tents in the square and for the Roman officials who were assigned to administer the registration. He charged the merchants, per head, what he normally charged per chamber, and required a minimum of four occupants per room. Those who were wealthy, like Aaron, the linen merchant, could have a private room. But they still had to pay as though there were four people occupying it.

Nathan gave the three Roman soldiers and the Centurion complimentary accommodations, but even they had to share one room. Four soldiers in one room produced its own set of problems. As tactfully as possible, Nathan told them that he wasn't responsible for the crowded conditions, and attempted to diffuse their dissatisfaction with a complimentary wedding jug of local wine, the pride of Bethlehem. The ceramic jug held thirty-two gallons of the rich red nectar. It had worked. Before the masses hit the city, the soldiers were appeased by the gift. Normally, Nathan liked the silence and the stillness of the mornings. He liked the world before the sun. But the morning headaches and distilled personalities brought on by the consumption of too much fermented grapes made for unpleasant sunrises during the early part of the count.

The one exception to the misery of this condition, was a young soldier named Sidrick. Sidrick was only five or six years older than Nathan's son, Caleb. He was decorated, and was second in command in Bethlehem. He didn't drink, and, during his stay, he had not made suggestive glances at Martha or Leah, as had the others. Sidrick quietly did his job and was curiously courteous, though reserved. Despite being garbed in the official uniform of a Roman soldier, which demanded the respect and apprehension of the Jews, he didn't flaunt his authority, nor did he hector people around. In fact, he was gentle and soft spoken, and this confused Nathan. There was something about his face, however, that looked tough and wary, as if he had run out of trust. Nathan was suspicious of Sidrick's manner. He was not comfortable with his attitude, and he was suspect of the young soldier because of it.

"I do not trust that young conscript, Sidrick," he told his wife in the privacy of their room.

"Why?" she asked. "He's certainly nice enough. He doesn't drink when he is off duty, and he doesn't grab at Leah and me like the rest."

"That's just it," Nathan responded. "I can trust my enemy because I know his motives and he is predicable. Sidrick is not like the rest, and I don't like not knowing him. I feel that he is up to something."

"Oh, Nathan, you don't trust anybody, especially if he is not a Jew," she said. "Perhaps he is restrained because he has a wife at home and he misses her. You were that way once."

"Just as well," Nathan said, discrediting Martha's intuition. "Keep an eye on him. I don't feel comfortable with him here."

Worrying was Nathan's way. He fretted about the weather, the cost of food, the scarcity of firewood, the money he managed to save, his piety, which he had little time for, the price of tuition for Caleb's residency at the academy, and the price of new clothes for Martha. To Nathan, the world was a vast quilt whose stitches were always coming undone. His worrying somehow worked like a needle, tightening those unsafe seams. If he could imagine events through their worst tragedy, then he seemed to have some control over them. He had an agony for every hour.

The stress of long hours and his guests' continual demands were beginning to work on Nathan, and Martha had seen it building. Nathan's grumbling had exceeded those of their guests and had begun to offend her and their small staff. When Martha offered to relieve him of his duties, and proposed that he should take a break from his tallies and their guests to walk to the market to buy fresh provisions, he jumped at the suggestion. The break, he thought, would allow him time to come down and visit with old friends he hadn't seen in a while. Martha expected that this break would be as much a relief for her as for Nathan.

When his wife made the proposition, Nathan jumped at it and said, "That's a great idea, Martha, I could use a break. But, before I go, I want to tell you something before I forget about it again."

"What is it?" asked Martha.

"I want to tell you about a dream I had last night," Nathan said, as she was leading him to the door. "I forgot about it until just now."

Just as Nathan was beginning to start to tell her about his dream, a guest came bursting through the open doorway, complaining about his wet blanket and his spoon which had been stolen. At the sudden interruption, and sensing a long discourse, Nathan turned toward his wife and said, "I'll tell you about it when I get back, Martha." He then darted out as the guest cranked up his displeasure, and began his escape to the square, leaving Martha to handle the problem.

The Innkeeper

Just as Martha had anticipated, Nathan was enjoying his walk alone to the market. He smiled as he mused over his decision to quadruple the daily rate for his rooms the day after the Governor of Syria, Quirinius, issued his order that complemented the mandate of Augustus that all in the country should be counted. He had already calculated that revenue-wise he had by this time made what the new tax increase would amount to, and he was sure that he was now in the pure profit range. This pleased Nathan. As he was thinking about it and relishing over this new opportunity to put some money away, an inner voice spoke to him regarding his stiff increases in the room rental rates. As he ambled on toward the market, he conceded that his rectitude bothered him some. Moving through the crowds, he began to argue with the inner voice, wrestling with the rationalization that he had earned the increase in rent because he was being run ragged, had little help, and was tired. To further support this position, he told his conscience that had the Roman officials given sufficient lead-time between their notice and the day the count began, he could have increased the size of his facility. Nathan was now trying to blame the authorities for his rate increase. His inner voice jumped at the contention and countered this reasoning with the conviction that had the officials given notice so that Nathan could have added on to the inn, he would have increased his prices, anyway. Wrestling with the conflict, Nathan ultimately agreed with the voice. He probably would have done exactly that. Weakly, he tried to argue back with the spin that due to the heavy workload, he had not had time to even visit his old friends who had set up their tents in the market, and he hadn't seen any of them since they first checked in. As he walked through the crowds and saw all of the people in the merchants' stalls, Nathan threw out a final argument to his inner voice that wouldn't let go of him. 'These merchants are making a bundle, too,' as if this would make things right and the voice would go away. He had put up a good argument, but as he finished shopping, he was still not convinced that he had won the inner discord.

Before the census-taking began, Bethlehem was a small town in terms of the number of people who lived and worked there. It was situated on a green, fertile hill and it looked across the plains at the Dead Sea. It was known for its olive wood, mother-of-pearl, embroidered goods, and papyrus used by the scribes in the Temple to replicate the teachings of Moses. Bethlehem was the final home of Ruth, her husband Boaz, and her niece, Naomi. Ruth, the wife of Jacob, was buried nearby just outside the city.

A rabbinical academy which sat on the summit of its highest hill was the only educational institution of Bethlehem. Caleb, Nathan's son, was among its students. More than half of the sitting Sanhedrin had graduated from the academy. Nathan had worked hard to get Caleb admitted to the school, and he was proud that a son of his was to become a member of the priesthood.

Bethlehem's government was two-layered. Herod was ruler of Palestine, it's Caesar. Since Bethlehem was in Syria, a Palestine province, Bethlehem belonged to Herod and his Roman soldiers. Herod made a wise decision when he allowed the Jews to superficially govern themselves, allowing a thin veneer of Jewish law granted to its citizenry by Roman license. He had made great efforts to mollify the Jews by publicly observing their laws, building them a temple, and reestablishing the Sanhedrin. But this liberty was tethered to Palestine with a short line. From his Roman perch in Palestine, the Jews were under constant hold and surveillance. As long as they recognized their freedom was controlled and they recognized Herod's ultimate authority, he allowed them to govern themselves, and that allowed him to use his resources elsewhere.

The Innkeeper

The Sanhedrin was a body of seventy-one Torah scholars presided over by the leader of the Pharisees. It had two chambers; one to preside over political and civil issues, and the other, the Great Sanhedrin, assumed the responsibility over the religious canons. The Sanhedrins were located a few miles away in Jerusalem, and functioned as a court. At the time, they served the Jews in much the same way the Papacy in Rome would later serve the Roman Christians, except they had Abraham and Moses as their leaders.

Nathan and his friend, Aaron, the linen merchant, both knew that the head count was only a preamble to the Caesar's new tax plan. There had been talk of it at the temple for weeks. Roman officials fed the temple managers just enough information to set the stage, but not enough to frighten them into talks of sedition, which would have been suicidal. Word of Herod's new tax plan had spread. But, unlike those who traveled far to Bethlehem with the knowledge that they would soon suffer an increase in their own taxes (and were worried about how they would secure new sources of revenue to pay them), Aaron and Nathan, like many of the other merchants, loved the droves of people filtering into the city. This business would certainly cover any tax increase they would likely receive. They were pleased with the Caesar's mandate.

As a linen merchant of great reputation, a procreator of the rare and expensive, Aaron had come to Bethlehem for the same reason as the other merchants: to offer his goods to the people coming for the registration decreed by the Caesar. He was Nathan's best friend, but, other than to say hello when Aaron had checked in, Nathan had had little time to visit with him.

After buying provisions for the inn, Nathan went to Aaron's linen tent to see his old friend.

As he entered his friend's tent, and before Nathan could even say "Hello," Aaron blurted

The Innkeeper

out, "I have to send word to Conrad, my associate, to send me some more silk and linen." The tent was large, held high with eight poles, and had three sides that touched the ground. Aaron went on without catching a breath. "It's good to see you, old friend. You would think by now I could gauge my inventory better."

Nathan started to speak but Aaron continued, "This business we are getting–I never would have guessed it would be so good! Hail to Herod! All of the local warehouses are full, and I have nowhere to stage my inventory except here in my tent. I will have to sleep here tonight to await its arrival and to guard my stock. I need four more camels and at least six more employees. Thank God for you, Nathan, my old friend, and thank God for your visit. Now I have someone to relieve me while I go relieve myself.

"Here, take this box, and hold on to it while I tend to nature's call," Aaron continued, handing the box to Nathan. "You don't know my stock and you don't know my prices, but if you get a customer while I'm gone–and you will–just delay him. Fill his ears with the elegant rubbish you feed your guests at the inn until I return. When I get back, I want you to tell me all about your family–Martha and your son, the rabbi."

Aaron hardly took a breath during his discourse and didn't listen for a response as he began to leave.

"Sure, go ahead," said Nathan. "But, hurry. I want to talk with you before I must return to the inn. I want to tell you about a dream I had last night. I am on a short leash because Martha is tending to the inn by herself. She is there all alone. I want to tell you about Caleb. So hurry."

Aaron stopped short of the tent's opening. "What about Caleb? Is there anything wrong?" he asked.

"Caleb is fine," Nathan answered. "He is at the academy finishing his last term under Rabbi Alterman. He's a good boy, but Alterman is strict and insensitive to what's going on here and how much I could use my son during this time. He won't release him to help."

"Nathan, hold that thought, and hold onto that box. I want to hear all about it, but I can't hold it myself," said Aaron, almost starting to run this time.

"Okay, but hurry!" Nathan yelled after him as Aaron took off on the fly.

"If I wanted to buy a bolt of white linen cloth, what would it cost me?"

The question startled Nathan. He turned from watching Aaron run down the dusty path. The soft voice didn't match the old figure that cast its shadow on the ground before him. The man was tall and tanned, his skin almost leathery in texture. He wore a full unkempt beard, and his hair matched it. Both needed tending to. "Why, it depends on the color and the texture," responded Nathan with the voice of authority.

"I said white," responded the gaunt, grubby man in an even softer voice, though he did not say it rudely. "Something that will wear well, that is soft and absorbent, and will stand up under frequent washing in the river. A cerecloth, perhaps. May I come in?"

"Sure," said Nathan. "Please do. We have fabric from all corners of the earth, in all qualities and all colors. If you tell me its intended purpose, perhaps I can suggest something suitable." Nathan was trying his best to delay this interested prospect and sound like he knew what he was talking about until Aaron could return. "What is your budget?" he added.

The soiled, disheveled man didn't respond. He was feeling the cloth to test its texture. He passed the expensive linen ephods, and occasionally he would stop, lift a bolt of linen, and rub it against his ear. His cheek was covered with a full beard, so he could not test the texture through the hair that coated most of his face. He slowly examined the linen, and it was a long while before he spoke again.

The noise throughout the marketplace-

combined with that of the animals standing on the other side of the walls–made conversation difficult. As Nathan waited for the man's answer, a second person entered the tent. He was obviously a rich man, dressed in fine clean linen and supported by a staff. The man stood six feet two inches and weighed over 250 pounds. He moved with purpose and carried himself with respect.

"Where is Aaron, the merchant of this tent?" the new man demanded.

"He will be back in a moment. May I help you?" Nathan answered.

"He's holding a box for us," the man said.

"Is this it?" asked Nathan.

"Yes. Did Aaron tell you what was in it?" the new, finely dressed man asked.

"No, he didn't, nor did he say that I could hand it over to anyone. You'd better wait until he returns."

"I am sorry, but that is not possible. I am in a bit of a hurry. I am Trasar, first attendant to Melchior, and I am here to pick up that box for the magi. The camel boy attending to

The InnKeeper

my transportation can't be detained much longer, and the authorities are not allowing camels in the marketplace today. I don't have time to wait."

"I am sorry, but I have no authority to release anything to anyone. You must be patient and wait until Aaron returns," Nathan replied.

"I don't think you heard me," interrupted the Trasar. "I am in a terrible rush, and even if I weren't, I couldn't wait in here with him." Trasar pointed his staff in the direction of the other man, who was still examining the linen. "He needs a bath, and what he is wearing needs to be burned."

Sarcastically, Trasar continued, "The public baths don't close for another hour. Of course, even with the luxury of a full hour, I doubt they can get him clean, nor will that box of olibanum you are holding."

"Olibanum? What is olibanum?" asked Nathan.

"Olibanum is frankincense. Mixed with myrrh, it is used medicinally and for fumigation. It is used in the temple to purify the sacramental offerings," murmured the old man in a soft voice. Standing at the rear of the tent, he was still fondling the cloth as he spoke.

Surprised that the transient could speak in such excellent Aramaic, and much more astonished that he knew what olibanum was, the magi's orderly turned to Nathan and said in an opined voice, "Surely a religious man like you knows what frankincense is?" With that question, the man turned and started to leave.

"Yes, I know what frankincense is. My son is to be a rabbi soon," Nathan replied emphatically.

"I'm sure you must be proud of him," said Trasar, "but I am out of time and have been inconvenienced long enough. Tell Aaron I was here." With that, the man turned and disappeared into the crowd.

Turning his attention back to the tousled man, Nathan said, "Now where were we?" Just then, Aaron entered the tent.

"Aaron! This is the last time…this man is looking for some cloth. Your need took much too long. Now I am out of time. I've got to run. Stop by the front desk when you close for the night, before you are ready to retire. It should be dark soon. We will have a cup of wine together. Oh, by the way, a man came in for this box, but you gave me no instruction regarding it, so I refused to give it to him. He left in a rush, unhappy at my unwillingness to hand it over."

"That must have been Trasar, Melchior's aide," Aaron replied. "Melchior sent word that he needed this olibanum today. I was his only source in all of Syria. It is too expensive for anyone else to carry. He paid for it in advance, in gold. It cost more than all of the cloth you see in my tent. He sent word that he would need it soon. As soon as the caravan arrives, I will send a runner to catch up with Trasar. I won't be coming back tonight, but hold the wine for me."

"All right, but let us spend some time together tomorrow." With that said, Nathan backed out of the tent. As he did so, he tripped over a lead rope that held the tent taunt and upright. While falling to the ground, he instinctively tried to break his fall, and, when he did, his foot got caught on the rope and he tore the strap off his left sandal. And, on his way to the ground, the stake that the rope was tied to, hooked on his shoulder bag. It snagged the strap, and when he fell in the opposite direction of the picket, the strap cut deep into his shoulder.

If Aaron had seen the cut in Nathan's shoulder, he wouldn't have laughed at him, nor would he have said, "Oh, the ineffable holiness of sudden events. Now that you are down, my friend, stay a while."

Nathan cursed as he got up. As he brushed off the dust, he painfully waved goodbye to his friend and hobbled through the stone-filled road, back toward the inn.

"Caleb, you might one day become a rabbi, but not through this academy, not now, anyway," said

The InnKeeper

Rabbi Alterman. The tribunal of priests sat unified in the expulsion action. "You were told," the Rabbi went on, "along with the others, when you first entered the academy, that a rabbi is to teach and to judge by the law you learn here. You are bright, Caleb, smarter than most in your class, but you are as undisciplined as a wild hare. Sympathy for others is encouraged, but empathy and personal connection is not. Detachment gives clarity of thought and allows decisions consistent with the laws. You are too penetrable to the difficulties of others. When Javan became stricken with the fever, and before he died, you should have been with the others in prayer, not in Javan's room holding his hand."

Rabbi Gamaliel and I talked to you about this when you were missed and then located," Rabbi Alterman continued. "But today you did it again when word came to us that Joel's brother had been killed unloading the heavy pottery from the caravan. You cut daven on the eve of the Sabbath, a pre-holy day, using only the excuse that Joel needed someone. You ran after him to the mount and stayed with him until we found you both. A rabbi is to lead, Caleb, to teach and to pray, leaving the mourning to others more suited to the delicacy of nurturing. A teacher's value is in the law, not in the lamentations of women."

Caleb looked nonplused at the rabbi as he considered the words he had just heard.

After collecting himself, he finally said, "Rabbi, we read that we ought to forgive our enemies, but we do not read that we ought to forgive our friends. Who is to forgive us if we do not join them in their sorrows? My education is giving me answers to questions that are not being asked. Even though I see evidence of it, it is hard for me to understand persecution and suffering. I do not come from a situation of poverty or oppression, and, even with the presence of Roman authority, we govern ourselves and are not like the others we represent; enslaved and marginalized.

THE INNKEEPER

Silence fell over the room. If there was an epiphany in his life, this was it.

Caleb went on, "While I find comfort in the stories of those who came before us, and their attachment to our ancestors, I feel the point of the Torah is not exclusively in our laws, or in the embodiments of our sacraments. At times, I feel that we have made an idol of the word of Moses when we make the words an end in themselves. Neither Abraham nor Moses met God in their study. The way I read the Pentateuch, they went out on their journey, and it was there, when they were among the people and among their problems, that they met the Lord. After their sojourns with our people, they returned to the Word of God for confirmation, and when needed, consolation. Truth is in the Word, but it is also in the faces and in the lives of our people. But we are not taught that. I feel that I must put myself in the sufferer's place to understand his suffering. I feel I must be formed, as well as informed."

"Silence! Enough! You have just validated our decision," said Rabbi Alterman. "When you keep rescuing people, you become the victim. Your thoughts are much in accordance with your inclination. Your discourse and speeches are not so much according to your learning, but to your infused opinions. When you wander from the law, you do so as a child does from the protection of its parents, and ignorantly, and dangerously, you take leave of your office. You wander indeed, and do not give heed to the demands that the law places on us, nor do you give notice to the requirements that we administer the law."

The rancor in Alterman's voice had reached a new zenith as he continued: "Rabbis are primarily teachers and interpreters of the Torah. We develop and maintain the liturgy, calendar, and other enlightened aspects of Judaism. This you elect to do out of your own choosing, and not because of any teaching of the Torah. Having a fruitful mind, you should not so much be compelled to know what to speak, as to find what to leave unspoken. Your tongue is as undisciplined as your nature. Rich soils are often to be weeded. It is now time to turn the earth. You have been warned. Your family is to be notified. You must leave the campus this afternoon, before nightfall. We are suspending you from your studies for a year until you mature and you are ready to resume."

"But–"

"No buts–that's all, Caleb. A man who cannot follow our laws cannot be expected to follow God's. Go clean out your room, and do not linger to bid farewell to the others."

The leather strap on Nathan's left sandal had broken when he had unwittingly backed over and tripped on the cord guideline that held a side post straight on Aaron's tent. To add injury onto injury, while walking home with his broken sandal in his hand, Nathan's exposed heel landed on a pile of large, serrated pebbles less than two hundred yards from the inn. With his first step after the bruise, excruciating pain shot through his foot and up his calf. So agonizing was the announcement of the injury, Nathan swore loudly as he fell a second time. The laceration on his right shoulder was now bleeding onto his tunic and his shoulder was throbbing almost as badly as his heel.

As Nathan picked himself up, limping and hurt, he was still cursing his pain and the luck that had befallen him. When he put his foot down to test his bruise, the pain was so great he fell again, this time on the bag he was carrying. He heard something break inside. Suffering from his shoulder and foot pain, he was trying to get up again when a hand reached down to help him. When he saw the extended hand, Nathan looked up and into the eyes of the old man who had been shopping for cloth in Aaron's tent. His face, with the sunlight behind it, seemed even more weathered and crusted than it had looked in the tent, but it was also con-

The Innkeeper

fusingly soft–almost as soft as the bundle of fabric the man had tucked under his other arm. The old man bent down, placed his free hand under Nathan's arm, and easily lifted him to a standing position. As soon as the man's hand touched his arm, a strange sensation ran through Nathan's body.

Once steady, the man dropped his hold and left his side without saying a word. Nathan called after him, "Just a moment. I want to thank you. What's your name?" The man never spoke and disappeared quickly into the crowd.

As he stood, Nathan felt a new energy in his body. He felt strangely young again. He took a tentative step, this time on the toes of his left foot. There was no pain. After he brought his right foot down next to the other, he took another step on the injured heel. Nothing. No pain. He put his full weight on the heel. Nothing. He stood for a moment, bewildered, trying to figure out what had happened.

Absently, he tossed the rawhide strap over

The Innkeeper

his injured shoulder, and he started to head for the inn, almost at a trot. Just as he got to the gate, he remembered the cut that opened the skin on his shoulder and the incision that went almost to his shoulder blade. He realized that he had placed the strap on the injured shoulder, but he felt no pain. He stopped and pulled off the bag's strap. The laceration from the strap cut had disappeared. There was no evidence that there had ever been an injury, except for the bloodstains on his tunic. Puzzled, yet excited, Nathan lifted his eyes heavenward and praised God for his healing. After his quick prayer of thanks, and as he entered the front door of the inn, he connected the old man with the healing. He stopped instantly in the doorway and turned to look for him, past the gate and into the crowds.

The stalls in the marketplace were jammed full of merchandise of all sorts–pottery, leather, papyrus, and ink stalls. Different varieties of wine, the main drink of the populace, were displayed in containers large and small. Canvas, linen, and ropes and twine of varying lengths and grades were popular items. Those who had purchased items but hadn't planned ahead for a way to carry them sought the stalls that sold bags, which were primarily made from hemp. The carpenter's tents offering chisels, hammers, clamps of varying lengths and sizes, dowels, laths, and lathes were filled with craftsmen looking at the latest implements to improve their projects. Each tent and stall owner, a master of enticement, vied for the attention of those passing through the market.

The baker's tent featured a large ceramic oven. With the aid of two mules and four burly men, the oven had been wheeled in on a pallet that had wooden wheels, just for the census count. Bread loaves of varying tastes and sizes were being sold to hungry people at prices three times the norm. This exploitation angered many, especially the poorer families, and a rancorous crowd had gathered.

The Innkeeper

A Roman soldier was summoned after several young boys ran through the baker's tent, grabbing what they could and scooting out the back when the baker and her helper bent down to take hot loaves from the oven. The soldier who responded to the call was Sidrick, the young, quiet officer who was staying at the inn.

Sidrick was unsympathetic as he listened to the baker's complaint, and he began to censure the merchant for beckoning him.

"Why do you call on us to protect you? If there is any thievery taking place here, you are the one doing the stealing. You, and the rest of the merchants who have raised your prices because of the crowds. You price your loaves so only the rich can afford to buy bread. A full denarius for a single loaf–that's a full day's wage for most of these people. You are the one who should be arrested, not the hungry who can't afford to buy your overpriced food and must resort to thievery in an effort to survive. You prey on the wounded."

The humiliated merchant became indignant at the rebuff, but, thinking it wiser, she contained her displeasure. Instead of suggesting to him that he enforce the law, she offered the soldier and his companions free bread. The soldiers were not on a per diem allowance, and they had to purchase food out of their own pockets, just like the travelers.

"The others might take you up on your offer, but I will not. You cannot buy my approval or my protection, as you steal from the pockets of those who cannot afford your food." With that, Sidrick turned and walked away, leaving the crowd at the baker's tent roaring with approval.

The naphtha lamps were being lit around the square, and in the homes in Bethlehem, as the sun finally scullioned its way behind the notch of Natailla, the smallest hill across the lake. Years before, as a child, Caleb had learned that the non-Jews believed Natailla was the bed of Amhor, the God of Light. To Caleb, who was sitting near the water's edge now, the day's conclusion wasn't coming easy. There seemed to be a struggle going on between the sun and Amhor. Either Amhor didn't want the sun to come home today and was fighting to keep him away, or the sun was like Caleb, and wasn't ready for home. Like the life in his friend's brother, the sun was refusing to leave quickly or quietly. Just as Esep, the sun appeared to have been hurt and, both, in the end, seemed to be crying out for deliverance from the pit before them.

Both deaths seemed painfully agonizing, but unlike Joel's brother whose death came loudly in screams of suffering, the sun's pain was declared in the colors it used to pronounce the agitation of its dismissal from the day. In a last attempt to maintain its presence, it threw itself like a spear above Caleb. It ricocheted its withering amber life across the sea before him and into the hill of the city to his back, in a seemingly desperate attempt to attach itself to anything that would hold it for a while longer.

Hours before the sun cut itself on the steep hill and bled into the city, Caleb had helped his friend and classmate, Joel, wrap his brother, Esep, in binding cloth and place the body in a provisional casket without a lid. They had laid him in a trough with his face up, and his eyes closed. The gawkers had long since vacated the side street where the camel caravan was being unloaded.

Even though Joel had grown up in Bethlehem and was now attending the academy, his parents had moved to Naia right after his registration. Naia was many miles away—an eight-day walk. Due to Jewish burial laws, Joel would not have enough time to notify his parents of Esep's death before he would be interred. He also could not send word tomorrow, for it was Saturday, the Sabbath.

Caleb and Joel were faced with two dilemmas. First, what would they do with Esep's body until burial? Second, who would recite psalms over Esep until the committal?

The Innkeeper

Rabbi Finberg said that he would officiate at Sunday's burial service, but insisted that Caleb immediately return to the academy for a meeting with the headmaster. They had to find a safe place for the body until Sunday. The city was overcrowded, and Joel, in his distress, couldn't decide what to do.

"Wait here Joel. I must go on to the academy and then I have an idea. I will get back to you as soon as I can," said Caleb.

After cleaning out his room at the academy, Caleb went straight to the inn.

Upon entering the courtyard, Caleb saw Nathan coming toward him. His father appeared unusually happy.

"Father, Father, I must speak to you!" Caleb yelled at him.

When they were close, Nathan asked, "Caleb, why are you not at the academy?"

"Father, Joel's brother, Esep, you know him, he was killed today while unloading the camel train behind the potter's shop. A load of jars fell on him as they were being lowered. One of the brace planks broke from its strapping. It ran through his chest as the entire load fell on him. He died a slow and agonizing death."

"Oh, my God!" Nathan cried. "I heard that someone had been hurt at the market, but I had no idea that it was someone we knew."

Abruptly changing the subject, Nathan continued, "What are you doing out of class?"

"Father, Father, never mind that for now. Listen. We can't bury Esep until Sunday, and there is no place to put the body until the burial. You must help us. We need to bring Esep here."

"Son, there is no place here. We are full to overflowing. As you can see, even the courtyard lacks space for a spare pot. Your mother and I sleep on the floor in the cleaning area, and Leah sleeps in one of the stalls in the barn. We have no space."

"Father, let me talk to Leah. I will ask her if we can keep Esep's body in the stall with her."

"Caleb, you can't ask her to do that."

"Father, please. We must help Joel. There is no other place to keep Esep. Let me talk to Leah."

The Innkeeper

Although he hadn't specifically thought about it, Caleb intuitively knew he was not going to return to the city that night. If it weren't for Leah, he wouldn't care to return at all. "By now," Caleb thought, "my parents know of my suspension. I can't face their disappointment on top of everything else that has happened."

With the exception of the fishermen's boats and nets spread out to dry, and a resting dog that took little notice, the shoreline was tranquil. Caleb hadn't noticed that he was alone; he hadn't noticed much of anything. He was not of this world; he was locked in an inner world of disillusionment and despair.

After the day's run, and after their gear had been cleaned, readied, and stored for tomorrow's first light, most of the fishermen had worked their way toward home. A few went to town to mingle in the city's excitement. Their catch had been brokered and sold long before their return, and demand had greatly exceeded the day's catch. They were anxious to get an early start the next day. Most had enrolled on the second day, and only a few were defying the edict.

The afternoon had grayed out; then, as if someone had thrown a switch, the world went crimson and magenta and gold. In anguish, Caleb had left Esep with Leah and Joel, both of whom were sobbing, and had gone to the shore.

Caleb absent-mindedly began to gather dry driftwood that had washed ashore as he walked above the water's edge of the beach. When he could carry no more, Caleb found a suitable place on the shore to build a fire. Sinking to his knees, he placed his bundle down. He then cleared a place, free of debris, and positioned some small pieces of wood into a pyramid. It took some time and effort, but Caleb managed to light a fire just as the last orange color on the city's buildings far behind him was painted over in a fresh gray pigment, and the first tear of twilight crusted on his cheek.

The absence of day does not necessarily

result in immediate darkness. Crepuscule, half-light, is the time of day that is set aside so that people can reflect on the hours just past, thank God for His blessings and protection, and pray for His keeping during the darkness that is to come shortly.

This was the eve of the Sabbath and the start of the holy day, and all tent managers and business owners were beginning to strap down and close their tent flaps in obedience to scripture law.

Even the gentiles, who had come in adherence to Herod's edict, would take notice and respect the rituals of the faithful.

Caleb was not ready to release the day, however, he had come full circle. He had started the day in prayer. Talking to God earlier consisted mainly of prayers of thanksgiving, petitions for the school, his family, and Leah. Now, he wanted to talk to Him again, but this time much differently. Now, with the fire burning brightly, and Caleb sitting next to it, looking out over the water, his anguish had turned to anger. This time he wanted to talk to God, man to man. He was crazed with emotion. As the flames of his small fire danced with the whiffs of the temperate wind that blew off the salted lake, Caleb began to unleash his hurt, his anger, and his bruises at God and at the way that God had managed the day. He was holding little back.

Caleb yelled out over the open waters, demanding, "If you are really there, God, come down here and talk to me like a man!" What have I done to fail you? What have I done to have your eyes cast away from me? Have I sinned? What have I done to you? Show me how I have erred, and I will be silent."

Caleb went on with a vengeance, "Can you see? Do you not have eyes? You are a coward who runs from your foul-ups and your mistakes, like the sun, but unlike the sun, which struggles to linger for a last look, you run and hide when called upon. What did Esep ever do to you, or to anybody, to warrant his death at this time, and why a painful one, as if he were being punished for an outrageous sin?

The Innkeeper

Caleb was crying now.

"Was it such a crime to work on the eve of a Sabbath, to want to feed himself?" Caleb continued in a rage. "He came at dawn today, to the temple, and, during davening, had asked you to forgive him for having to do so. Are you such a despicable God that you would have our people starve just so we can pay homage to someone who won't even come and talk to us? Why did you take our fathers out of Egypt just to watch us die?"

"Where is the integrity in your pledge to Moses?" Caleb cried out over the still waters. "If you are so fainthearted, send down one of your angels to defend you. Why do I have to shout into the wind to one who does not take notice?" Caleb was shaking, the adrenaline rush had taken over.

Caleb went on: "What did I do to warrant dismissal from your temple, other than to share in the wounding devastation of a friend? I am glad I have been expelled. I believe in You, but I don't understand You, nor do I understand what You want from me.

It is important to think and to reason, but I think it is also important to be led by the heart. You made me what I am, and who I am doesn't fit. While I believe in the prophets and in the laws of Moses, and I believe this is where we find the answers to life, I also feel that I can see You, and discern your desire, in the hearts of your people. Sometimes, what I see, and what I read, are in conflict. What I see now is an indifferent, whimsical, and purposeless God."

Caleb's body was tight with passion. His biceps were taut, sinewy, and beads of sweat covered his arm. He slumped to the ground. With a clenched fist stretched toward the dim, emerging stars, he bellowed his hurt heavenward and then dug his fist into the sand. Tears were streaming down his cheeks. His pain matched, and may have even exceeded, the physical suffering of Esep, except it hadn't come from broken bones in a depressed chest or from a lance that entered his breast. His heart and his spirit were broken. The pain is the same.

The Innkeeper

Out of exhaustion and disillusionment, Caleb stopped the tirade. The spit and crackle of the fire, an occasional faint sound coming from the city behind him, and the splash of a meandering wave as it found its place on shore, were all that Caleb could hear. He did not receive an answer to his questions. The wind had joined the sun.

Sitting there, looking out on the waters, Caleb saw an old man appear, out of the corner of his eye, walking the beach toward him. Caleb ignored him, turning his face away from the approaching figure. The last thing he wanted to do was to enter into a conversation with anyone–except God. He waited for the man to pass to continue his monologue with the faceless God.

When the old man got closer, he called, "Caleb?"

At the sound of his name, Caleb turned toward the old man. He waited a moment until the man got closer, and replied, "Yes, my name is Caleb. What do you want?"

J. Sid Raehn

"What are you learning?" asked the old man.

Caleb did not answer the question.

"I hope I have not found an opportunity to learn lost to a presumption of sufficient knowledge," added the old man.

Caleb sat looking, quizzically, at the figure standing before him.

"I was sent to find you," the man said.

"By whom, my father?"

"Well, not exactly," replied the old man.

"By whom then, and what do you want?"

"I was sent to tell you a story."

"A story? I don't need a story."

"Thank you, Caleb," the man said, ignoring Caleb's disinterest. "I think I will sit down. It's been a long day."

The old man looked soiled, his hands were rough with calluses, and his clothes were worn. Caleb thought, "What could this man possibly tell me?"

"Sit, Caleb. The story is a short one. It is good that you have not let the authority of another define who you are, but I want you to listen to what I have to say."

The Innkeeper

The old man began,

※

"*A long time ago in my village*, a young fugitive came to us seeking asylum. The authorities were after him for a crime he said he didn't commit. After a brief meeting, we were willing to take him inside and hide him. When the soldiers arrived in search of the fugitive, my people protested and said we knew nothing. Suspecting that we were lying, the soldiers warned that unless the fugitive was turned over by morning, our entire town would be destroyed."

"Deeply fearful, we rushed to our rabbi for counsel. Our teacher, greatly troubled with our situation, started searching scripture for the answer to our predicament. All night he read, and found nothing. Then, just before dawn, his eyes fell on a passage, '*It is better that one man should die for the people, than the whole people be lost.*'

"He was sure that he had found the answer, and he came to us with the news of his finding," the old man continued. "When the soldiers returned, they were informed that the fugitive was indeed hidden among us, and the young man was taken away. We threw a big party in the town, lasting far into the night, and we celebrated our deliverance by the grace of God."

"But our pastor returned to his study, still troubled. An angel appeared to him and asked, 'What's the problem?' 'I still don't feel right about turning over the fugitive,' the pastor told the angel. The angel replied, 'Did you not know he was the Messiah?'

"The pastor was incredulous. 'The Messiah! How was I to know?' he asked."

"'If, instead of reading your Bible, you had taken the time to visit the young man and had looked into his eyes, you would have known he was the Messiah,' the angel replied."

※

When he finished telling the story, the old man stood, placed his hand on Caleb's shoulder, and said, "Caleb, you have a good heart, and one day you will be a fine rabbi. In life, there is a bouncing back of things; if you have deep sorrow, then you must have great joy. Continue to study the Word of God so that you will know how to conduct your affairs and lead others to know Him, but never pass judgment on a man without looking into his heart, through his eyes. Soon, you will have an advocate with the Father whom you call God."

When he had finished, the old man walked away, leaving Caleb near the fire to contemplate the meaning of what he had just heard.

Some time later, the last flicker of a small flame in the dying fire danced for a long second, almost defiantly, as it seemed to grasp at the last chance of life.

Caleb was exhausted as he tried to piece together the old man's story and the events of the day. With the darkness as his blanket, he slipped into a deep, narcoleptic sleep, curled next to the shallow, warm pit.

Moments into his slumber, Caleb began to dream. He dreamed that he saw a man walking across the Dead Sea holding the hand of a small boy. The boy was Joel's younger brother, Esep. Esep was waving at him and smiling.

Sometime in the night, a bright light appeared in the now darkened sky, but it was way off in the distance. Caleb lay asleep, facing the East. As the light began to glow more brilliantly, the power of its brightness pierced Caleb's eyelids and he began to stir. Following a few moments of discomfort, and upon resurfacing from the depths of unconsciousness, Caleb opened his eyes.

The light was like a lightning bolt, bound for earth, yet steady, and its purpose like a search light in reverse. It hit the earth far off in the distance, but it was a bright white and it lit up the sky. Caleb squinted and looked directly at it. The beam seemed to be coming from a star. He stood, silently staring at the light, wondering what it was, and what it meant. As he raised his arm and pensively looked toward the pageant of the whitish beam, the clamp that held the passion of the

The Innkeeper

day to his heart released itself, and the emotions that brought Caleb to the shoreline began to fade as this new concern took its prerogative.

"What is this?' he wondered aloud. "And, what is it shining on?" Then, he deciphered the direction of its movement. The powerful light was moving slowly toward him.

It was late in the afternoon when the nondescript couple arrived at the gates of the city.

"I am sorry, but you must leave the animal outside the city," announced the gatekeeper.

"Sir, we have traveled far this day and my wife, as you can see, is heavy with child," said the man, who stood with a tired, but beautiful young girl who sat on a donkey. "We must be allowed to enter and find lodging."

"Yes, I can see your situation, but I can do nothing more than follow my orders. You may enter, but the mule must remain outside."

"But, sir, the walk through the square and to the inn is a long one. Perhaps an exception, due to her condition, can be made."

"I am sorry, but I have no—"

"Let them pass," a voice said. Both men turned to see who dictated the order. A Roman soldier, a Centurion, stood in the afternoon shadows just beyond the gate.

"Your name, sir, so that I may thank you for your kindness," said the young man, as he held the donkey's lead rope.

"The name is Sidrick, but I have no need for appreciation. You may pass."

The young lady straightened and said, "Bless you, Sidrick. May God take a liking to you, and may your days be long and sweet."

"Pass now before you start a commotion that I cannot stop," Sidrick responded.

As they passed through the gates, people noticed that an exception had been made, and they began to murmur among themselves.

Mary and Joseph wound their way past the tired tent merchants who were busy securing their wares for the night. They only stopped once to ask for directions to the inn.

Nathan and Martha were at the counter when the couple arrived at the inn. The courtyard was already beginning to fill, and the cook fires, thanks to Jonathan, had been kindled. The tarps that gave shelter to the ground guests gave way to an occasional breeze. They flapped easily in the wind as the thermals lifted them and then reversed themselves.

"I am sorry, but, as you can see, we have no room. There isn't so much as an inch to be given, even in the courtyard," Nathan told Joseph. Leah entered as Nathan was speaking, and noticed the couple and the condition of the woman still on the donkey.

"Nathan," said Leah, "they may have my space in the stall. I will only need to find a place for Esep's body."

"But where will you stay?" replied Nathan.

"It doesn't matter. I am going to look for Caleb. He hasn't returned, and I don't know where he has gone. At any rate, they may have my bed," said Leah.

The InnKeeper

"What about Aaron's room?" Martha interjected. "He's not coming back tonight. He must stay and guard his tent."

"His room has already been committed," Nathan responded crassly.

"To whom?" questioned Martha.

"Never you mind to whom, it has been taken."

"Nathan, this lady is with child. She needs a room!" barked Martha.

"We have no room. They may have Leah's stall, if she is willing to give it up, and that's it," said Nathan.

"Please, come with me," Leah gestured to the couple. "It is getting late. Let me take you to my stall before it gets too dark to see. I will light the lamp and make arrangements for the removal of the young boy's body who shares it."

"Thank you," said Joseph as he began to follow. "My name is Joseph and this is Mary. We've come a long way."

"My name is Leah," she responded, as she led them to the stall area.

"Who is praying over this boy?" Joseph asked, seeing the open casket.

"No one yet," said Leah. "No one is here except me and I cannot."

"Then, I will," said Joseph.

"He is in heaven now," said Mary, as the young girl and Joseph moved the makeshift coffin to one side of the stall. As Joseph knelt by the body of the young boy and assumed the ancient role of the *T'hillim Yid*, he began to recite psalms of faith over Esep's still body.

"Heaven?" asked Leah. "Where is that?"

"It is where God is and where angels live," answered Mary.

"I do believe in angels," Leah said, "They are messengers sent by God to deliver His messages to the ordained ones. But we–I do not believe in a heaven. Sheol perhaps, but we do not know of a place called heaven. Life for us ends when it ends. I am surprised that you don't know that. This has been a sad day. Please do not make light of it."

"Please forgive me, Leah, I did not mean to offend you," said Mary.

"The one I'm pledged to is wrought in despair," Leah continued. "His best friend's

The Innkeeper

brother lies here dead. Because of Caleb's own kindness, he has been expelled from the academy. We have no future. And, there is no future after death."

"Leah, once you find your Caleb, you must return with him and stay with us this night. It will be cramped, but the warmth of closeness will kill the chill and I have something to share with you both," said Mary to Leah. "There is a future for you both. There is a future for us all. Go now and find your Caleb." Just then, a sharp pain erupted inside of Mary, and she gasped and doubled over, clutching her stomach.

"Please, go quickly and fetch us some water and a blanket, if you can find one," said Joseph to Leah.

Joseph quickly took off his coat, laid it on the ground, and gently guided Mary upon it. He then grabbed the coarse blanket that had softened her ride from Nazareth, and put it under her head as a pillow.

J. Sid Raehn

Leah ran to the inn to get a water jug, and then ran to the well to fill it. When she arrived at the well, she was unnerved to find a long line of water-seekers ahead of her. She began to ask others to allow her to break in, explaining her mission. No one offered their place in line, for they had been there for some time.

"Please!" she pleaded. "The water is not for me. I am from the inn and we have a mother with child who is about to deliver. Please let me go to the front of the line, for her sake." No one moved. She began to cry.

An older man, with a coarse beard and filthy clothes, approached her. He had a jug of water in one hand, and a bolt of cloth under his free arm. "Here, take these my child," he said, as he handed her his water and the soft, white cloth. "I will wait in line, fill your jug and bring it to the inn."

"Thank you, oh, thank you," Leah cried. "This cloth is so soft. It must be expensive. A baby will be wrapped in it. Are you sure you want me to take it? You may not get it back."

The Innkeeper

"Yes, I know," said the old man, in a warm, wry voice.

"Who are you?" asked Leah.

"A friend."

"But I have never seen you before."

"Yes, you have. You just haven't noticed. Now go."

"Please, before I go, I must know your name so I can tell the couple about the person who gave them the cloth."

"I am the same one who is watching over your Caleb. Now go." With that, the old man turned and took his position at the end of the line.

When Leah returned to the stall, there were just moments to spare. Mary was in full labor. Joseph had already dumped the feed from a trough and had cleaned it as best he could. Without saying a word, Leah arranged the cloth in the trough and then ran with the jug to the inn. She poured water into a ceramic bowl and took the bowl to the courtyard to heat it over a cook fire that was already going strong. While it was warming, she ran back

The Innkeeper

into the inn's small kitchen. She grabbed a knife, a half-loaf of bread, a blanket, and the largest piece of smoked fish she could find. She didn't want Nathan to see her, only because she didn't have time to explain. She rushed to the stall and deposited the load, and then ran back to get the bowl of warmed water.

Leah took the knife and cut the long sleeve off the left side of her dress. She dipped it into the water and placed the warm, wet cloth on Mary's forehead. Once she had cleaned her face and wiped the beads of perspiration, she took the knife and removed her right sleeve from her dress. This time she used the material, now warm with fresh water, to prepare for the child.

Leah noticed that Mary also wore long sleeves and was puzzled by it.

"Sidrick?"

"Yes, Commander?"

"You have acted quietly and strangely

these past few days. Do you think I have failed to notice?" asked the commander of the Roman contingency assigned to keep the order in Bethlehem.

"I hope I have not given you reason to be alarmed, Commander," replied Sidrick.

"Well, you have, and yet you haven't," said his leader. "Your work has been excellent as usual, but you haven't been with us in spirit. You are here, doing a good job, but you are not here. What's going on with you? And, why are you asking for the gate assignment each day, a duty our juniors dislike?"

"My allegiance is with the Caesar of Rome, and my orders come from you, Sir," Sidrick replied. "Nothing has changed. I take my life and my service to Rome seriously."

"Yes, I know of your allegiance, Sidrick, and you are a fine officer. I am due for a transfer soon, and I have written the garrison commander about your performance. I wouldn't be surprised if you were promoted and transferred to Rome."

"Thank you, sir, but I hope it doesn't come soon."

"Why is that so?" asked the commander quizzically.

"Both my wife, Deborah, and our daughter are with the fever and I cannot leave until–until whatever becomes of them. I have had someone with them around the clock for three days and I have been at the gates most of these days waiting for the caravan that is to bring the medicines. But, as yet, they have not arrived."

Just as Sidrick was talking, an aide came to the door and beckoned the commander. "You have a visitor, sir–a citizen–a sullied one."

"Excuse me, Sidrick," and the commander rose from his chair and left with his aide. Minutes later, he returned. "From what I have just heard, I don't think the caravans will be needed, Sidrick," the commander told him.

"Why do you say that? What do you know, sir?"

"Collect yourself, Sidrick. A scroungy old Jew just left a message that you should return home now. The fever, your wife and child had, has broken, and they are doing fine. But, before you go tearing out of here, tell me how your relationship with these people is so good that they should send one of their own to you, as a friend, with this good news."

"I don't know any of these people, and I don't know who you are talking about," said Sidrick, bewildered. The puzzled commander let Sidrick go.

Caleb was fully awake now. The stream of light was moving toward him. He did not know what time it was or how long he had been asleep. In his wonder, and in his fear of the light, he had already forgotten the visit from the stranger who had sat with him. He began to run back to the city.

He was still running as he passed the stables on his way to see his father.

"Leah! What is going on here, and what has happened to your dress?" Caleb exclaimed. He stood motionless and con-

The Innkeeper

fused. "Does this mean…are you no longer clean?" he asked, looking forsaken.

"She is as pure as the fresh snow on the mountains," a voice came from the shadows. The same strange man who had been on the beach with Caleb and had met Leah at the well, emerged from the darkness.

"Oh, it's you again," said Caleb. "What are you doing here, and what is going on?"

The old man approached, and he held a new linen dress with full sleeves.

"Please let Leah go put on this new garment, for she has been pleasing—"

"Pleasing to what, to whom?" Caleb demanded.

"Caleb, let her pass, and come with me," replied the old man.

As Leah disappeared into a dark corner to change her dress, the old man led Caleb to the space usually occupied by Leah. The stall was softly lit by the single lantern that hung just inside the stall. A man, woman and child were there.

"Joseph, Mary, this is Caleb," the old man

said as he introduced Caleb to the couple. "Caleb is a student from the academy, and he is studying to become a rabbi."

"Caleb," said the old man, "this is their new child, born this night, here in the stable, with the help of your Leah. Her sleeves were used to wipe Mary's brow and to clean the new baby before they wrapped him in linen and put him in the manger."

Caleb sighed at the news.

"Hello, Caleb," said Joseph. "Leah has told us all about you. We are sorry about your friend's brother, but you will, one day, see that he is alright. Since you are a rabbi, will you say a prayer for our child?"

"I am not a rabbi. Up until today, I was a third-year rabbinical student, but I was expelled from the academy only this afternoon," replied Caleb.

"Yes, we heard," said Mary, "but we have been asked to allow you say a prayer for our child."

"Who asked you?" charged Caleb.

"The man who brought you here," replied Mary.

The Innkeeper

Caleb turned to the old man. He was gone. Caleb stared into the darkness. The stables at the inn faced east. As he looked into the darkness for the old man, he noticed that the star, and the beam of light that emitted from it, had moved closer to Bethlehem since he left the seashore. "Do you see that star over there?" asked Caleb.

"Yes, we do," replied Joseph.

"What do you make of it?" asked Caleb.

"I think it is telling us that you should bless this child before he gets any older," answered Joseph.

"But I am not ordained. You need a real rabbi."

"A rabbi is one in whom the sacraments are entrusted, and one who is a teacher," said Mary. "Whether you realize it or not, Caleb, you are both of these. You love the Lord and we are told that the Lord loves you. Your ordination is not of this world. It is much greater."

"You realize that no matter what I pray, it won't be as good a prayer as one from the mouth of a fully educated priest?" asked Caleb.

J. Sid Raehn

"Yes, we know. That's why we want it from your heart, not your head," said Joseph.

Just then Leah appeared, looking as beautiful and as radiant as the mother holding the child. "Come Leah, hold my hand as I whisper the prayer I have been saving for our own child," Caleb summoned.

As Caleb knelt before the infant, he gently placed a hand on his forehead. The child was sleeping peacefully. Caleb began to softly pray aloud:

❀

"Watch over this thy child, Oh Lord, as his days increase; bless and guide him wherever he may be, keeping him unspotted from the world. Strengthen him when he stands, comfort him when discouraged or sorrowful, raise him up if he should fall and in his heart, may thy peace which passeth understanding abide all the days of his life."

❀

Just as Caleb was about to stand, the baby stirred, yawned, stretched, and awoke. At the instant their eyes met, Caleb knew who was looking at him.

In sheer excitement, Caleb jumped up and tried to yell out. But no sound came from his mouth. He tried again, but he was mute. He became frightened. He turned to Leah and tried to say something to her. Nothing. He tried to scream. No sound. He fell to his knees, buried his face in his hands, and began to cry. No sound could be heard, but tears ran down his cheeks. Leah knelt and put her arms around him. She was tormented by what she saw before her.

The old man emerged again from the shadows. "Caleb," he began gently, "for the next few days there will be many visitors who will come to see this child. That star will continue to move this way until it stops here on this spot. It is leading the way for the people who follow it. When you rise, you will be able to speak, but you will not be able to remember what you saw in the eyes of the child. The time has not yet come for Him to be announced to the world."

"Tomorrow you will return to the academy," the old man continued. "The hearts of the administrators will be softened, and they will take you back. After a while, you will be elected to the Sanhedrin, where you will become a judge. You will be called on again, and your eyes will be made to see, but not today. Do you understand?"

Caleb shook his head to say that he did not understand.

"You will, in time," said the old man. "Now rise."

As Caleb stood, the old man disappeared again into the night.

"Leah?"

"Yes, Caleb?"

"Can you hear me?"

"Yes, I can," Leah said with excitement. "What did the man mean, Caleb, about the eyes of the child?"

"What man?"

"The old man that was right here a

The Innkeeper

moment ago–the one who gave me this dress," replied Leah.

"I remember the old man and him giving you that dress. I remember him disappearing right after he brought me to your stable."

"No, Caleb. He was just here and he talked to you about the baby's eyes."

"All that I can remember," said Caleb, "is after I gave the child our prayer, I was struck dumb. I remember falling on my knees and praying, and now I am standing here talking to you as if nothing happened."

"The hour is late," Joseph interrupted. "Leah, thank you for all that you did to help Mary deliver our child. And Caleb, thank you for your prayer. I do not think your words will be lost to the world. Now, Mary and I have to get some rest, and you do too."

Nathan and Martha lay on their blanket, exhausted from the day. As Martha settled in, she said, "Nathan, before you fall asleep, I want to discuss some things with you. I can't believe that Caleb was suspended from the academy. Will you go see the Rabbi tomorrow?"

"Yes, I fully intend to, after I speak to Caleb," Nathan replied with earnest.

Martha continued, "With all the bustle of the new people coming here to see that baby in the stall, it is strange that none of them asked for a room. I guess they knew there were none to be had. That light from the star is certainly a boost to our image and to our standing within Bethlehem, and is causing quite a commotion. I hope all this attention will not come back to haunt us. If it weren't for Sidrick's quick return to the city, after visiting with his family, we would have been in real trouble. He had a way with handling the crowds. He seemed happy, as if he were a different person. Remember, I told you he was a good person, even if he is a Roman," Martha continued.

"But, before you comment, this morning–it seems like ages ago now–before the guest with the blanket problem, and just before you left for the market, you were about to tell

The Innkeeper

me of a dream you had last night. Do you still remember it well enough to tell me about it now? Also, can you tell me why, in heaven's name, you kept Aaron's room empty when that poor couple with their new baby out in that chilly stable could have used it? You knew Aaron was not coming back tonight."

"The amazing part of the dream, Martha, was its clarity. I understood it completely," Nathan said. "Every detail of it was so alive and crystal clear. Yes, I remember it, down to the smallest detail, which is another unusual thing. Usually, most of my dreams are like smoke; they evaporate within minutes of my wakening. Yes, I remember it, but as it turns out, even with all the commotion that I thought had a bearing on it, even with that star's light, it wasn't as prophetically accurate as I thought it was this morning."

"What are you saying, Nathan?" Martha asked.

Nathan ignored her and went on. "I had hopes for it even into this evening, and it was because of the dream that I kept the room open. I dreamed that our prayers had been answered–the prayers of all of our people. With each hour of the day, I felt more strongly that the dream would be fulfilled. The stranger in the market today who healed my foot and shoulder, the star... I felt that these were all signs that my dream would become a reality. I dreamed, Martha, that we had a new king–mightier than any king this world has ever known. A real honest to goodness great king, one that would rule all of the earth, not just Rome, and that he would be staying with us here, at the inn, tonight. That's why I kept that room open."

The InnKeeper

Afterword

I did not totally write what follows. Part of it was e-mailed to me by a friend who read part of the *InnKeeper* manuscript. My story was just that—a story. Their's is not. I hope my story caught your heart. I hope theirs touches every fiber of your being.

"*There was no room in the Inn.*" I wonder about the Innkeeper in your story, Sid, and what happened to him. I wonder how he must have felt when he found out who had knocked at his door. "If only the older fellow had given me a clue as to who they were, surely I would have…"

We all would. If Billy Graham, James Earl Jones, Colin Powell or Sister Teresa, knocked on my door, cold and hungry, I not only would have fed them and saw to it that they were bathed, and had fresh clothes, I would have given up my bed and sheeted it with my finest linen. Maybe because it would make me feel important. Maybe just so I could tell others that "Lincoln" slept here.

It is ironic that he came not for kings who would have provided for Him succor and comfort, whose station allowed relief and privilege, but for the InnKeepers whose lives were full with the busyness of the census registration, taking place in our town.

I guess we all are InnKeepers, of sorts. Most of us live behind freshly painted solid core doors, that not only provide us shelter from the elements, but also provide for the safety of the artifacts descriptive of a life well managed. We are definitely busy with our own census activities-- those things we care about--busy with meaningful tasks, and busy with some things we wished would just go away and find a haven under some other roof. In most of our homes, there is a room set aside for guests. We keep it cleaned and unsullied for the right guest. Mostly, it just sits there waiting for the next dusting.

I don't think that if I did get a knock on our door, it would be from the hand of

The Innkeeper

Joseph, asking for shelter for him and his wife, well with child. In fact, I doubt if it would be from the hand of any great king, even though I live in a castle worthy of one. And the street people don't come down our road, a neighborhood of nice houses, knocking on doors, so they will not pose an inconvenience on a busy evening.

As we should, we sing heartily the familiar songs that announce the reason for the season, with cups of warm cider and mulled wine, surrounded by friends and family. We thank God for our blessings, securing for us a place in history that is void of hunger, oppression, disease, and leaving us a life without escape or hope - all behind the door of our Inn.

We are truly blessed - just as was the Innkeeper. With the power to open our door or keep it closed.

We have fought hard to escape and to disengage ourselves from the painful parts of our past. We successfully climbed from our pit and don't even want to look back down to survey from whence we came. The views below are too racking to even want to revisit the moments of our yesterdays. We will save that for our therapist. We made it! We passed many as we ascended, momentarily pausing on each rung to catch our breath and to contemplate our next move. Try as I might, some comfort is naturally felt as I compared my flight to the flight of others, giving credit to my tenacity and to my hard work as the cause of my comfort - laziness and sloth the cause of their annulled trajectory.

Perhaps, all of these are the cause of my success and are also the cause of the failure of others to reach the elevation of my flight path. But I still stop for a moment and thank Jesus, before I sleep, for the part He played.

Fleetingly, I recognize the agony of others. It is unveiled to me in the warmth and comfort of my living room, cloaked in the warmth of my fireplace, as NBC and CBS draw my attention to it on the six o'clock news. I close my eyes briefly to thank God that we, my family, are as blessed as we are, and that He has spared us—that we are not among them. I wonder if this was a door opened, closed at the push of the remote control, as I run into the kitchen to remove the cookies from the oven.

Are we still charged as keepers of our door? Are we to be graded on how, and, if we open it? Who will we let in? How much will they require? Will it take from me that which comforts me? I have many coats in my closet - each one for its own occasion.

This door thing has me worried. I don't want to go down in history as a postscript. I want to be a major player. But, alas, I am like the Innkeeper who wouldn't recognize Jesus from the many I pass daily, doing what I am good at—taking care of myself.

I think when my time comes, I would rather be like the shepherds who, in their obtuseness, heard a multitude of angels singing and telling me what was happening and what I must do. With something as bang-fulness as this was, I knew I would do the right thing, and as directed, go to visit Him, earning my place, albeit, without the effort of personal discernment, in history. I just don't want some stranger to knock on my door, when I'm taking clothes out of the drier, and while I'm mentally preparing myself for a job interview.

Christmas to the shepherds was as it is to all of us–practically unavoidable. Christmas to your InnKeeper, however, was just another day of hope and unrealized grace.

THE INNKEEPER

ACKNOWLEDGEMENTS

The first person I want to thank is my wife, Happy, who read and re-read this manuscript more times than I did, or cared to. She liked the story. She believed in it and she believed that it could have happened just as I told it.

At first she was afraid to change anything, except the words that were spelled differently than Merriam Webster would have them. She held fast to her position and didn't equivocate in her editing even when I tried to convince her that an educated man could find more than one way to spell a word.

Next, I want to thank our oldest daughter, Shannon, for two things. She, unknowingly proved to me, without a shadow of a doubt, that prayer does work, if it is in God's plan, and she proved that there are angels who watch over special people. Secondly, as an English major, she encouraged me to write, and her own convictions gave me the courage to step out and write from my heart, rather than from my head.

I want to thank our youngest daughter, Brittney, who most certainly could have been Leah.

Lastly, I want to thank those along my journey who have been a part of the cliché, "When two are gathered, you will have three opinions." In my frustration and desire to understand, I eventually found faith.

–Dr. J. Sid Raehn

The InnKeeper

Give the First Gift of Christmas

This year, share the true meaning of Christmas. Give your loved ones a gift they will always remember—a signed copy of My Story's very special edition of *The InnKeeper*.

To place your Christmas order, please call My Story Publishing at (850) 668-5846 and they will ship it directly to your loved one with a gift card from you. There is no charge for shipping and handling.

To receive an 8x10 copy of Caleb's Prayer for your child, a grandchild, a child of a relative, or a friend's child, you may do that also by calling (850) 668-5846.

Lastly, if you are on the net, you may order your additional copies of *The InnKeeper* and/or Caleb's Prayer, by writing to us at MyStoryPub@aol.com.

Coming in 2002-3

Poignant, Classic. Dr. J. Sid Raehn's enthusiastically awaited sequel to The InnKeeper, *The LawKeeper*.

Order your 8 x 10 copy of

Caleb's Prayer

From *The InnKeeper*

Watch over this thy child, Oh Lord, as his days increase; bless and guide him wherever he may be, keeping him unspotted from the world.

Strengthen him when he stands, comfort him when discouraged or sorrowful, raise him up if he should fall and in his heart, may thy peace which passeth understanding abide all the days of his life.

Call My Story Publishing at 850-668-5846 or write MyStoryPub@aol.com

Calligraphy on parchment. Ready for framing. The perfect gift to a special child.